Shake the Tree!

minibombo

• First U.S. edition 2018 • First published
in 2015 by minibombo, Italy, as *Dalla chioma* by Chiara Vignocchi,
Paolo Chiarinotti, and Silvia Borando • Illustration: Silvia Borando •
Published in English by arrangement with minibombo, an imprint of TIWI
s.r.l., Via Emilia San Pietro, 25, 42121 Reggio Emilia, Italia. • minibombo
is a trademark of TIWI s.r.l. © 2015 by minibombo/TIWI s.r.l. • Library
of Congress Catalog Card Number pending • ISBN 978-0-7636-9488-3 •
This book was typeset in Tisa Pro Regular and Medium. • The
illustrations were created digitally. • Candlewick Press, 99 Dover Street,
Somerville, Massachusetts 02144 • visit us at www.candlewick.com
Printed in Heshan, Guangdong, China • 17 18 19 20 21 22 LEO 10 9 8 7 6 5 4 3 2 1

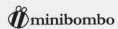
CANDLEWICK PRESS

Check out **www.minibombo.com**
to find plenty of fun ideas for playing
and creating inspired by this book!

Mouse spots a nut.
"Mmm," she says.
"I'm going to gobble that up!"

So she shakes the tree
a little to the right . . .

shake

and a little to the left.

shake, shake

UH-OH.

"Mmm," says Fox.
"A scrumptious mouse."

"I'm going to gobble you up!"

So Fox shakes the tree
to the left . . .

shake, shake

and to the right.

shake, shake, shake

UH-OH.

"I'm going to gobble you up!"

Warthog shakes the tree
to the right . . .

shake, shake, shake

and to the left.

*shake, shake,
shake, shake*

UH-OH.

Bear shakes the tree to the left . . .
shake, shake,
shake, shake,
shake, shake

and to the right.

shake, shake, shake, shake, shake, shake, **SHAKE**

"Mmm," says Bear.